Bertie's Escapade

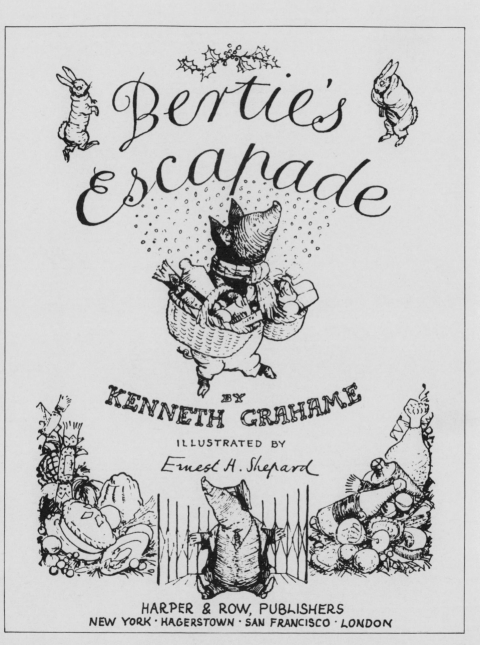

Bertie's Escapade

BY
KENNETH GRAHAME

ILLUSTRATED BY
Ernest H. Shepard

HARPER & ROW, PUBLISHERS
NEW YORK · HAGERSTOWN · SAN FRANCISCO · LONDON

It was eleven o'clock on a winter's night. The fields, the hedges, the trees, were white with snow. From over Quarry Woods floated the sound of Marlow bells, practising for Christmas. In the paddock the only black spot visible was Bertie's sty, and the only thing blacker than the sty was Bertie himself, sitting in the front courtyard and yawning. In Mayfield windows the lights were out, and the whole house was sunk in slumber.

"This is very slow," yawned Bertie. "Why shouldn't I *do* something?"

Bertie was a pig of action. "Deeds, not grunts," was his motto. Retreating as far back as he could, he took a sharp run, gave a mighty jump, and cleared his palings.

"The rabbits shall come too," he said. "Do them good."

He went to the rabbit-hutch, and unfastened the door. "Peter! Benjie!" he called. "Wake up!"

"Whatever are you up to, Bertie?" said Peter sleepily.

"Come on!" said Bertie. "We're going carol-singing. Bring Benjie too, hurry up!"

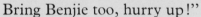

4

Peter hopped out at once, in great delight. But Benjie
grumbled, and burrowed down in his straw. So they hauled
him out by his ears.

Cautiously they crept down the paddock, past the house, and out at the front gate. Down the hill they went, took the turning by the pillar-box, and arrived at the foot of Chalkpit Hill. Then Benjie struck.

"Hang it all," he said. "I'm not going to fag up that hill to-night for anyone!"

"Then I'll bite you," said Bertie. "Choose which you please."

"It's all right, Bertie," said Peter. "We're none of us going to fag up that hill. I know an easier way. You follow me."

He led them into the chalk-pit, till they stood at the very foot. Looking up, it was like the cliffs at Broadstairs, only there was no band at the top and no bathing-machines at the bottom.

Peter pulled out a large lump of chalk and disclosed the entrance to a long dark little tunnel. "Come on!" he said, and dived in; and the others followed.

2

They groped along the tunnel for a considerable way in darkness and silence, till at last they saw a glimmer of light; and presently the tunnel ended suddenly in a neat little lift, lit up with electric light, with a seat running round three sides of it. A mole was standing by the door.

"Come along there, please, if you're going up!" called the mole sharply.

They hurried in and sat down. "Just in time!" said Peter.

"Any more for the lift?" cried the mole, looking down the tunnel. Then he stepped inside smartly, slammed the door, pulled the rope, and they shot upwards.

"Well, I never!" gasped Bertie. "Peter, you do know a thing or two, you do! Where—what—how—"

The lift stopped with a jerk. The mole flung the door open, saying "Pass out quickly, please!" and slammed it behind them. They found themselves standing on the fresh snow, under the open starlit sky.

They turned round to ask the mole where they were, but the lift had vanished. Where it had been there was a square patch of grass free from snow, and in the middle of the patch was a buttony white mushroom.

"Why, we're in Spring Lane!" cried Bertie. "There's the well!"

"And here's Mr Stone's lodge, just in front of us!" cried Peter.

"Splendid!" said Bertie. "Now, we'll go right up to the house, and sing our bewitching carols under the drawing-room windows. And presently Mr Stone will come out, and praise us, and pat our heads, and say we're dern clever animals, and ask us in. And that will mean supper in the dining-room, and champagne with it, and grand times!"

They hurried up the drive, and planted themselves under the windows. Then Bertie said, "First we'll give 'em 'Good King Wenceslas'. Now then, all together!"

"But I don't know 'Good King Wenceslas'," said Peter.

"And I can't sing!" said Benjie.

"Well, you must both do the best you can," said Bertie. "Try and follow me. I'll sing very slow." And he struck up.

Peter followed him, as best he could, about two bars behind; and Benjie, who could not sing, imitated various musical instruments, not very successfully.

Presently they heard a voice, inside the house. It was Mrs Stone's, and she was saying, "What – on – earth – is – that – horrible caterwauling?"

Then they heard another voice – Mr Stone's – replying: "It sounds like animals – horrid little animals – under the windows, squealing and grunting. I will go out with a big stick, and drive them away."

"Stick! O my!" said Bertie.

"Stick! Ow, ow!" said Benjie.

Then they heard Mrs Stone again, saying, "O no, don't trouble to go out, dear. Go through the stable-yard to the kennels, and LET – LOOSE – ALL – THE – DOGS."

Dogs, O my!" said Bertie.

"Dogs, ow, ow!" said Benjie.

They turned tail and ran for their lives. Peter had already started, some ten seconds previously; they saw him sprinting down the carriage-drive ahead of them, a streak of rabbit-skin. Bertie ran and ran, and Benjie ran and ran; while behind them, and coming nearer and nearer, they could hear plainly

Wow – wow – wow – wow – wow – WOW!

Peter was the first to reach the mushroom. He flung
himself on it and pressed it; and click! the little lift was
there! The door was flung open, and the mole, stepping
out, said sharply: "Now then! hurry up, please, if you're
going down! Any more for the lift?"

Hurry up indeed! There was no need to say that. They flung themselves on the seat, breathless and exhausted; the mole slammed the door and pulled the rope, and they sank downwards.

Then the mole looked them over and grinned. "Had a pleasant evening?" he inquired.

Bertie would not answer, he was too sulky; but Peter replied sarcastically: "O yes, first rate. My friend here's a popular carol singer. They make him welcome wherever he goes, and give him the best of everything."

"Now don't you start pulling my leg, Peter," said Bertie, "for I won't stand it. I've been a failure to-night, and I admit it; and I'll tell you what I will do to make up for it. You two come back to my sty, and I'll give you a first-rate supper, the best you ever had!"

"O ah, first-rate cabbage-stalks," said Benjie. "*We* know your suppers!"

"Not at all," said Bertie earnestly. "On the contrary. There's a window in Mayfield that I can get into the house by, at any time. And I know where Mr Grahame keeps his keys – very careless man, Mr Grahame. Put your trust in me, and you shall have cold chicken, tongue, pressed beef, jellies, trifle, *and* champagne – at least; perhaps more, but that's the least you'll have!"

Here the lift stopped with a jerk. "Tumble out, all of you," said the mole, flinging the door open. "And look sharp, for it's closing time, and I'm going home."

"No you're not, old man," said Bertie affectionately. "You're coming along to have supper with us."

The mole protested it was much too late; but in the end they persuaded him.

When they got back to Mayfield, the rabbits took the mole off to wash his hands and brush his hair; while Bertie disappeared cautiously round a corner of the house. In about ten minutes he appeared at the pigsty, staggering under the weight of two large baskets. One of them contained all the eatables he had already mentioned, as well as

apples, oranges, chocolates, ginger, and crackers. The other contained ginger-beer, soda-water, and champagne.

The supper was laid in the inner pigsty. They were all very hungry, naturally; and when everything was ready they sat down, and stuffed, and drank, and told stories, and all talked at once; and when they had stuffed enough, they proposed toasts, and drank healths – "The King" – "Our host Bertie" – "Mr Grahame" – "The Visitors, coupled with the name of Mole" – "Absent friends, coupled with

the name of Mr Stone" – and many others. Then there were speeches, and songs, and then more speeches, and more songs; and it was three o'clock in the morning before the mole slipped through the palings and made his way back to his own home, where Mrs Mole was sitting up for him, in some uneasiness of mind.

Mr Grahame's night was a very disturbed one, owing to agitating dreams. He dreamt that the house was broken into by burglars, and he wanted to get up and go down and catch them, but he could not move hand or foot. He heard them ransacking his pantry, stealing his cold chicken and things, and plundering his wine-cellar, and still he could not move a muscle. Then he dreamt that he was at one of the great City Banquets that he used to go to, and he heard the Chairman propose the health of "The King" and there was great cheering. And he thought of a most excellent speech to make in reply – a really clever speech. And he tried to make it, but they held him down in his chair and wouldn't let him. And then he dreamt that the Chairman actually proposed his own health – the health of Mr Grahame! – and he got up to reply, and he couldn't think of anything to say! And so he stood there, for hours and hours it seemed, in a dead silence, the glittering eyes of the guests – there were hundreds and hundreds of guests – all fixed on him, and still he couldn't think of anything to say! Till at last the Chairman rose, and said, "He can't think of anything to say! *Turn him out!*" Then the waiters fell upon him, and dragged him from the room, and threw him into the street, and flung his hat and coat after him; and as he

was shot out he heard the whole company singing wildly, "For he's a jolly good fellow – !"

He woke up in a cold perspiration. And then a strange thing happened. Although he was awake – he knew he was awake – he could distinctly hear shrill little voices, still singing, "For he's a jolly good fe-e-llow, and so say all of us!" He puzzled over it for a few minutes, and then, fortunately, he fell asleep.

Next morning, when Miss S. and A. G. went to call on the rabbits, they found a disgraceful state of things. The hutch in a most untidy mess, clothes flung about anyhow, and Peter and Benjie sprawling on the floor, fast asleep and snoring frightfully. They tried to wake them, but the rabbits only murmured something about "jolly good fellows," and fell asleep again.

"Well, we never!" said Miss S. and A. G.

When Albert King went to take Bertie his dinner, you

cannot imagine the state he found the pigsty in. Such a litter of things of every sort, and Bertie in the midst of it all, fast asleep. King poked him with a stick, and said, "Dinner, Bertie!" But even then he didn't wake. He only grunted something that sounded like "– God – save – King – Wenceslas!"

"*Well!*" said King. "Of all the animals!"